By Melissa Spencer

For my wonderful nieces

Artwork by Prettygrafik Design
A-Z of Fairy Wishes is part of the
Fairy Wonderland range at
www.merryelfmas.com

Once upon a time in a fairytale, a King invited all the fairies in the land to celebrate the birth of his baby daughter.

The fairies each offered their gifts of

BEAUTY, WIT, GRACE, DANCE, SONG AND MUSIC.

To cut a long story short, the princess grew up, was saved by a handsome prince and lived happily ever after.

Nowadays, fairies realise that girls are far too important to wait around for Prince Charming.
Modern girls can lead exciting lives, where they can be whatever they want to be, and do what makes them feel happy.

The fairies in this book have come together to bring you their

of wishes to help girls become the heroes in their own stories.

A
Live a life
full of
dventure

Be Brave

Be Confident

Dream Big

Remember you are
Enough

Be Friendly

Be Generous

Be Happy

Trust your
Instincts

Join In

Be Kind

Love
Learning

Believe
in
Magic

No Regrets

Keep an
Open-Mind

Follow your
Passions

Questio
Everythin

Respect
Yourself

Reach
for the
Stars

Try your Best

Be Unique

Make your
Voice Heard

Spread your Wings

EXpect
Wonderful Things

Believe in Yourself

Face
Challenges
with Zest

We send our wishes to help you make the story of your life

Printed in Great Britain
by Amazon